Mickey's Young Readers Library • Mickey's Young Readers Library • Mickey's Young Readers Library • Mickey's Young Readers Library

This Book Belongs to:

VOLUME
16

Mickey and the Troll

STORY BY DIANE NAMM

Activities by Thoburn Educational Enterprises, Inc.

A BANTAM BOOK
NEW YORK · TORONTO · LONDON · SYDNEY · AUCKLAND

ISBN 0–553–05631–X
Published simultaneously in the United States and Canada. Bantam Books are published by Bantam Doubleday Dell Publishing Group, Inc. Its trademark, consisting of the words "Bantam Books" and the portrayal of a rooster, is Registered in U.S. Patent and Trademark Office and in other countries. Marca Registrada. Bantam Books 666 Fifth Avenue, New York, New York 10103.
Printed in the United States of America
0 9 8 7 6 5 4 3 2 1
A Walt Disney BOOK FOR YOUNG READERS

One day, Mickey was walking through a small village high in the mountains. Mickey smiled as he looked around. "This village is perfect," he said with a sigh. "Nothing could ever go wrong in a place like this."

The town was so lovely that Mickey decided to stop a while and have some lunch. As he waited for his food, Mickey overheard the worried voices of an old man and old woman at the next table.

"Excuse me for listening," Mickey said, leaning toward the two. "But is something the matter? And is there anything I can do to help you?" he asked in a kind voice.

"My, what a nice young man you are," said the old woman.

"Yes, but I don't see how you can help us," added the old man, shaking his head sadly.

"Please let me try," said Mickey. "What's wrong?"

The old woman began to explain, "We have owned a small sheep farm near the village for many years. But the last ten years have been bad for us and bad for the sheep."

"Why is that?" asked Mickey. "Everything looks so peaceful and lovely here."

The old woman and old man looked at each other. Then they told an unhappy tale.

"Ten years ago, this was a busy village. There were lots of happy young men who lived and worked here. We hired many of the young men to tend our sheep. But after just a few weeks of tending sheep, each young man would disappear," the old woman said sadly.

"You mean they just left?" Mickey asked.

"No," sighed the old woman. "But we did think that at first."

"I don't understand," said Mickey.

The old woman continued, "When the young men all disappeared, the villagers said it was because of the troll who lives at the edge of the forest near our farm."

"But what does the troll have to do with the disappearing young men?" Mickey wanted to know.

"We don't know, but that is the only reason anyone can think of to explain why the young men have disappeared," the old woman said sadly.

"Now no one will work for us because of the troll. We are too old to care for our sheep, so we are going to lose our farm," added the old man.

"Maybe I can help," said Mickey. "I'll take care of your sheep until you can find someone else to tend them. I'm not afraid of a troll."

"Oh, thank you," smiled the old man. "That will help us save our farm."

And so Mickey went with the old man and old woman to their farm. They showed him the green, grassy fields where the sheep were grazing.

Mickey looked around at the beautiful sight. Then he noticed the trees at the edge of the meadow. He had never seen trees like that before.

Mickey wanted to ask about the trees, but it was getting dark, and the old man and old woman looked very tired. It was time to go.

That night, the old couple made Mickey feel right at home. They gave him a large bed to sleep in, with nice soft pillows and a warm quilt.

The next morning Mickey woke up to the delicious smells of breakfast.

As Mickey ate, the old woman packed a picnic lunch for him to take to the meadow. The old man dusted off his wooden staff to give to Mickey. He had made it himself and had used it long ago to tend his sheep.

Mickey took up the staff and his lunch and went on his way.

By noon, Mickey was hot and hungry. He decided to have lunch in the shade of the tall trees. As he ate, he looked at the fluffy white sheep grazing on the peaceful hill. It was hard to believe that a mean, ugly troll could live in such a lovely place.

After lunch, Mickey was thirsty. "I sure do wish I had a cool cup of water," he said out loud.

As if by magic, a gray stone well, with clear, cold water appeared before Mickey's eyes!

"Where did that come from?" Mickey wondered. "I didn't see a well here before."

Mickey looked around, but there was no one in sight.

"Well, I am thirsty," Mickey said to himself. Then he walked over, staff in hand, to get a cup of water from the well.

Mickey leaned over to pull up the pail, resting the wooden staff on the edge of the well. As he pulled on the rope, he knocked the wooden staff down.

Looking into the deep well, Mickey knew he would never be able to climb down and get it back.

"Oh, no!" he cried. Mickey thought about how the old man had made the staff himself.

Before he could decide what to do next, an ugly little troll with bright red hair came running out from behind one of the trees. Mickey could see that the troll was angry.

"Get away from my well!" shouted the troll. "I know what you're up to—you want to steal my treasure! Get out of here, before I really lose my temper!"

Mickey couldn't believe it. The stories about the troll were true! But Mickey answered calmly. "I don't want your treasure. But I would like to have my wooden staff back. It fell into your well by accident."

"Oh, so all you want is your little old staff. Is that it?" asked the troll.

"That's right," Mickey replied.

"Well, we'll see about that!" said the troll, diving down into the well.

"Is this the staff you dropped into the well?" the troll asked, with a sly grin. He held up a bright bronze metal staff. The troll was hoping that Mickey would tell a lie and answer "yes." Without taking more than a second to answer, Mickey said it was not.

The troll stopped grinning. Muttering to himself, he disappeared back down the well.

In a few minutes, the troll reappeared. This time he had a shiny silver staff. As he climbed up out of the well, he asked Mickey again, "Is this the staff you dropped into the well?"

Mickey looked at the staff. He knew it was worth far more money than the plain wooden staff that the old man had given him. But once again, Mickey told the troll that this was not the right staff.

Mickey's answer made the troll very angry. With a growl, the troll hopped back into the well.

One more time, the troll climbed out of the well. This time he was holding a beautiful golden staff. He pushed it into Mickey's hands and asked, "Is this the staff you dropped into the well?"

But once again, Mickey said it was not. And he would not take the golden staff.

Mickey's honest answer made the troll so angry that he turned a deep purple and let out a terrible roar. Then the troll dove back into the well, and in a puff of green smoke, both the well and the troll disappeared.

Mickey blinked his eyes, trying to see through the smoke. He looked over at the trees near the edge of the meadow. For a moment, he thought the trees were moving.

"Hmmm," he said to himself. "Must be the troll's smoke in my eyes." Then he blinked again. "Why, it almost looks like those trees are turning into . . . people!"

And believe it or not, that was just what was happening. Those tall trees weren't trees anymore. They were tall, young men, holding staffs and shaking leaves and branches from their heads and their arms.

When the young men saw Mickey, they rushed over to thank him for breaking the troll's spell.

"But how was the troll able to turn you all into trees?" Mickey asked.

The young men hung their heads. No one wanted to tell.

At last, one of them said in a low voice, "We were not honest like you were. When we dropped our wooden staffs into the well, as you did, we pretended the troll's staffs were ours."

"Once we did that, he turned us into trees," another spoke up.

"I see," said Mickey. "I sure am glad I told the truth!"

Then the young men thanked Mickey and headed for their homes. They were eager to get back to their families and to the village where they had been so happy before the troll had made them disappear.

As Mickey watched them go, he saw the four staffs lying on the grass. Mickey picked them up. Then he went to gather in the sheep to take them home.

The old man and woman were very happy to see Mickey return safely from the meadow. Mickey explained how the troll was gone for good and the young men were now safely back with their families. The couple could not thank Mickey enough. Then he handed them the four staffs. With the money they could get for them, they need never worry about losing their sheep farm again.

"Is there any way we can repay you for everything you have done?" the old woman asked.

"I'm just happy I could help," Mickey replied.

From that day on, all the people of the village lived happily, and honestly, ever after. And the troll was never seen or heard from again.

A Picture Tale

How well do you remember this story? Read the sentences below, and fill in the missing words. Use the pictures in the clue box to help you. (Hint: Some words may be used more than once.)

Mickey met an old couple who lived on a ______ farm. While Mickey was taking care of the sheep, a ________ suddenly appeared. Mickey dropped his ________ into the well. All of a sudden, from out of nowhere came a ________ who was very angry at seeing Mickey near his ________. Mickey told the ________ about dropping the ________ into the ________. Three times the troll went into the well to get Mickey's ________. But the ________ tried to trick Mickey, and so he came up with three different ________ instead.

Do you remember what happens next? How did Mickey triumph over the troll?

After your child does the activities in this book, refer to the *Young Reader's Guide* for the answers to these activities and for additional games, activities, and ideas.

The True Picture

Look at the three pictures below. Only one of them shows the truth about the story you just read. Can you figure out which one it is?

What A Colorful World!

The mountain village where the story takes place is very colorful. How many different colors can you find in this picture? Name something that is the same color as each of the words in the box.

green	blue	yellow	white
purple	gray	brown	red

Where's The H ?

In this story, Mickey triumphs over the troll because he is honest. The word *honest* begins with the letter *h*. You can't hear the letter *h* when you say the word, but you can see it. Look at all the *h* words below. Point to the words in which you cannot hear the *h* sound.

Young Readers Library • Mickey's Young Readers Library • Mickey's
Readers Library • Mickey's Young Readers Library • Mickey's Young
Young Readers Library